This book belongs to

_____

but I'll let you read it
because you're nice.

Creative Director: Tricia Legault • Editor: Gayla Amaral

Manufactured by Lyrick Studios, Inc. under license from Humongous Entertainment, Inc. Distributed in the U.S. by Lyrick Studios, Inc.
Printed in China. No part of this publication may be reproduced, stored in a retrieval system or transmitted, in any form or by any
means, electronic, mechanical, photocopying, recording or otherwise, without prior written permission of the publisher.

1 2 3 4 5 6 7 8 9 10   01 00

ISBN 1-57064-948-0

Library of Congress Number 00-100701

FREDDI FISH™
THE MISSING LETTERS MYSTERY

Written by
Dave Grossman

Illustrated by
Jay Johnson

Freddi Fish and her best pal, Luther, were in Salmon City to visit their friend Brook Stickleback.

"Look at all the neon lights!" exclaimed Luther.

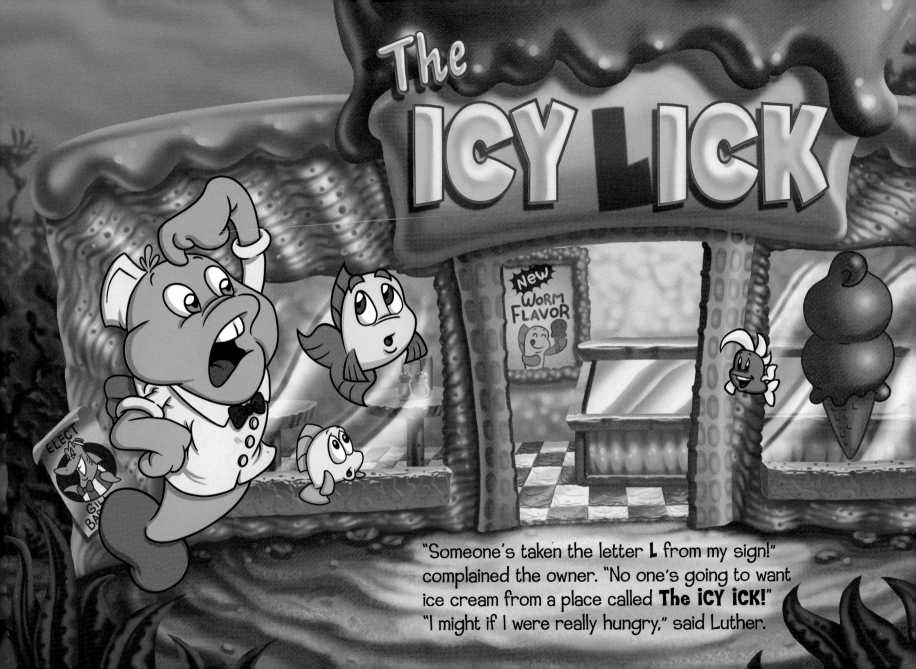

The ICY LICK

New WORM FLAVOR

ELECT GILL BA...

"Someone's taken the letter **L** from my sign!" complained the owner. "No one's going to want ice cream from a place called **The ICY ICK!**"
"I might if I were really hungry," said Luther.

They found Chief Pike with Mayor Fishhook, who was throwing a fishy-fit because his sign was missing letters, too!

RE-ELECT MAYOR FISHHOOK

HE'S ALL HEART

"It's supposed to say 'He's all **HEART**'- not 'all **HAT**!'"

"How am I supposed to beat Gill Barker with a sign like that?!" said Mayor Fishhook. "We've got to get to the bottom of this!"
"Yes, sir!" said Chief Pike.

"Maybe we can help," offered Freddi.
"I'm pretty good at mysteries."
"I can use all the help I can get,"
said Chief Pike.
"Chief Pike, there's trouble at the
FLIGHT SCHOOL!" yelled a policefish.

"Thank goodness you're here," said the flight school instructor. "My **L** is missing, and those sardines outside think this is a **FiGHT** school."

FLIGHT SCHOOL

"Who do you think took your letter?" asked Freddi.
"Well, Stylish Rob the Barber was here earlier," answered the flight instructor.
"Maybe he has a clue!"

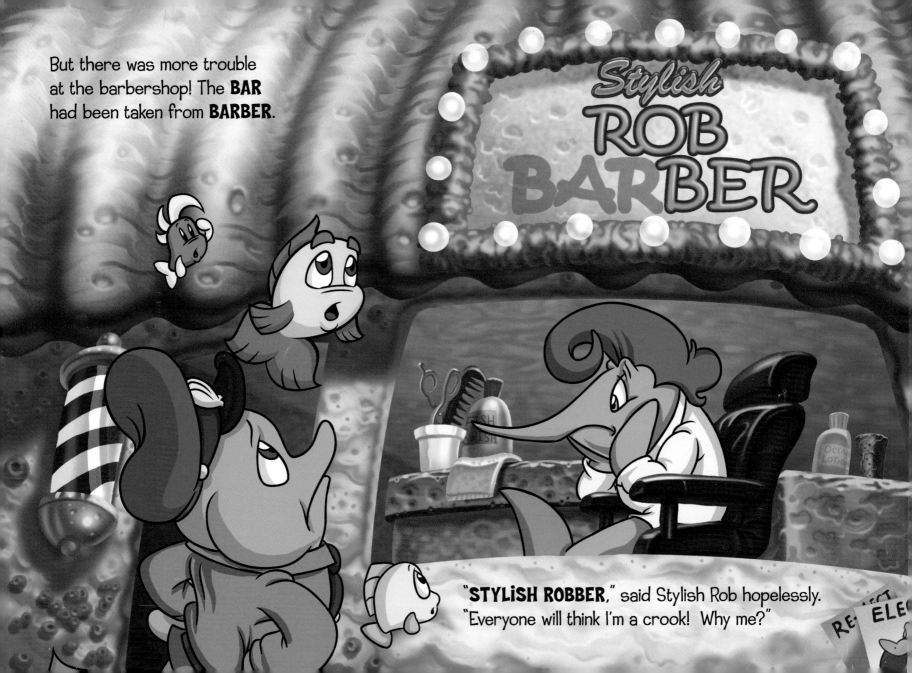

But there was more trouble at the barbershop! The **BAR** had been taken from **BARBER**.

Stylish
ROB
B**AR**BER

"**STYLISH ROBBER**," said Stylish Rob hopelessly. "Everyone will think I'm a crook! Why me?"

"That's a good question," said Freddi. "If we knew **WHY** the thief was taking these letters from the signs, that might help us figure out **WHO** it is."

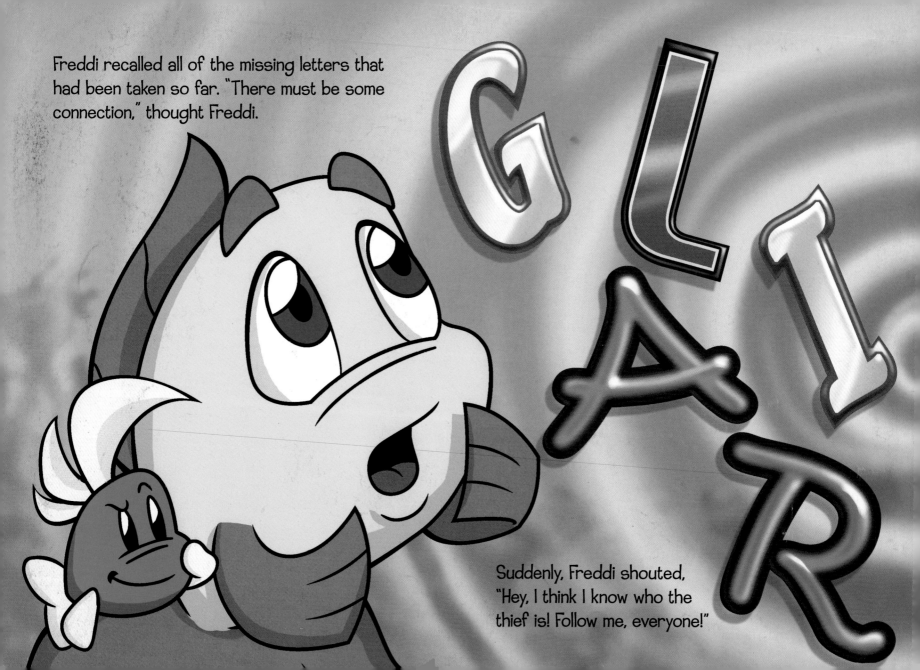

Freddi recalled all of the missing letters that had been taken so far. "There must be some connection," thought Freddi.

Suddenly, Freddi shouted, "Hey, I think I know who the thief is! Follow me, everyone!"

Freddi and her friends took a taxi crab to **THE RUSTY SKiPPER** restaurant. They arrived just as someone was taking the **K** from the sign! Freddi jumped out of the taxi crab. "Stop thief! Hold it right there!"

"How did you figure out it was me?" asked a startled Gill Barker. "Simple," said Freddi. "The missing letters spelled **G-i-L-L B-A-R-K-E-R**, just like your election flyers. Only the letter **K** was missing, and then I remembered that **THE RUSTY SKiPPER** had the biggest **K** in town!" "I guess spelling out my name WAS a tip-off," sighed Gill. "I wanted a big, flashy sign just like Mayor Fishhook's."

"Besides, I didn't think anyone would notice the missing letters," said Gill. "We noticed because the signs spell different names now," Freddi pointed out.

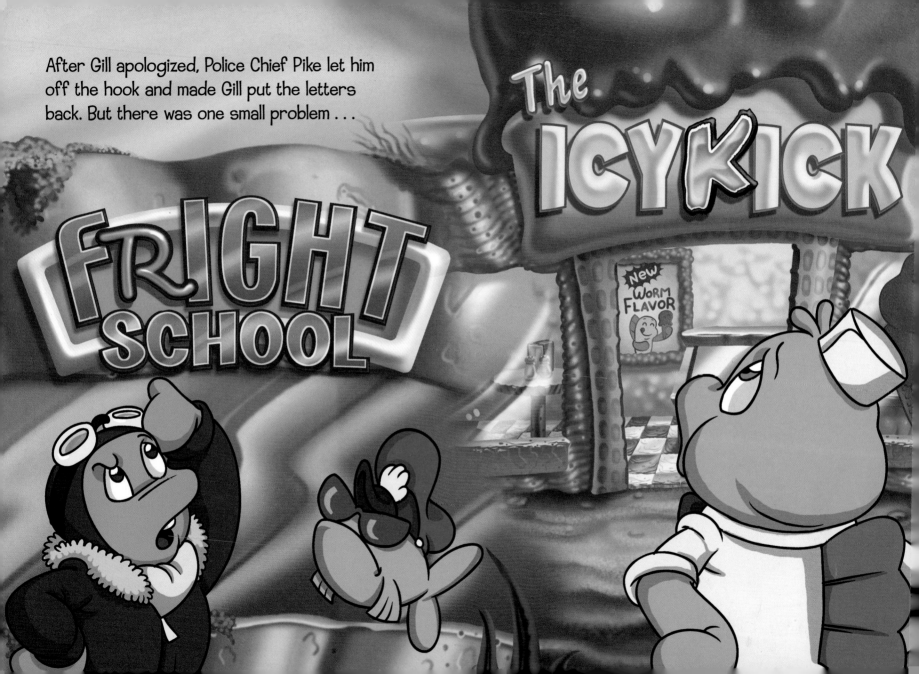

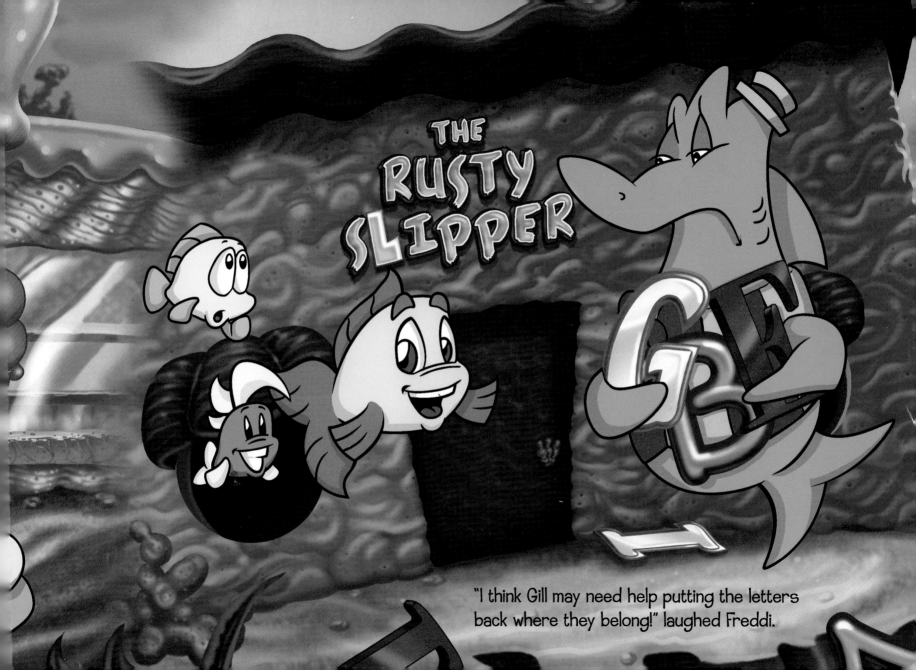

THE RUSTY SLIPPER

"I think Gill may need help putting the letters back where they belong!" laughed Freddi.